The Further Adventures of Nick Tickle, Fairy Tale Detective

by Steph DeFerie

Baker's Plays
7611 Sunset Blvd.
Los Angeles, CA 90042
BAKERSPLAYS.COM

THE FURTHER ADVENTURES was originally staged by the Chatham Middle School Drama Club in 2008. The first performance was on December 12 at the Chatham High School Auditorium, Cape Cod, Massachusetts with the following cast:

GRANNY POSSUM . . . . .Ryan Leach
QUEEN CUPCAKE . . . . .Meredith Biron
MAGIC MIRROR . . . . Taylor Wilkins
SNOW WHITE . . . . Rachel Wallace
VINNIE . . . . Max Arvidson
EVE . . . . .Brianna Donahue
PEARL . . . . .Jasmine Squires
PRINCE CHARMING . . . . Jon Morse
BLUEBEARD . . . . .Mike Couto
NICK TICKLE . . . . John Mulholland
PUSS . . . . Libby Nickerson
RUMPLESTILTSKIN . . . . Liam Phelan
MRS. STILTSKIN . . . . .Alena Hunt
FAIRY GODMOTHER . . . . .Allie Jason
CINDERELLA . . . . Joyce Higashi
JANE . . . . .Jessica Alcocer
GERT . . . . .Caroline Couto
PIRATES . . . . Nick Matsik, Joyce Higashi, Jessica Alcocer

The play was performed again on December 31 at the Chatham Drama Guild as part of the town's First Night Celebration with the following cast:

GRANNY POSSUM . . . . .Chloe Murphy
QUEEN CUPCAKE . . . . .Whitney Knowlton-Wardle
MAGIC MIRROR . . . . .Makayla Cussen
SNOW WHITE . . . . .Grace Reilly
VINNIE . . . . Max Arvidson
EVE . . . . .Caroline Couto
PEARL . . . . .Sam McIntosh
PRINCE CHARMING . . . . Liam Phelan
BLUEBEARD . . . . Nick Matsik
NICK TICKLE . . . . .Mike Couto
PUSS . . . . Cassie Meservey
RUMPLESTILTSKIN . . . . Liam Phelan
MRS. STILTSKIN . . . . Emileigh Perkins
FAIRY GODMOTHER . . . . Max Arvidson
CINDERELLA . . . . .Alena Hunt
JANE . . . . Haley Rae
BERT . . . . .Travis Carroll
PIRATES . . . . John Mulholland, Jasmine Squires, Haley Rae
Travis Carroll

Both productions were directed by Karen McPherson. The sets were designed and built by John Kaar, Keith Phelan and Jackie St. Thomas. The costumes were provided by Betty Marshall. The lights were run by Kevin Couto.

CAST OF CHARACTERS

OLD GRANNY POSSUM, a narrator
QUEEN CUPCAKE, an evil queen
THE MAGIC MIRROR
SNOW WHITE
VINNIE, a huntsman
STEVE (or **EVE**), a dwarf
MERLE (or **PEARL**), a dwarf
PRINCE CHARMING
BLUEBEARD, the pirate
A BAND OF PIRATES
NICK TICKLE
PUSS IN BOOTS
RUMPLESTILTSKIN
MRS. STILTSKIN
FAIRY GODMOTHER
CINDERELLA
GIANT (voice only)
WAYNE (or **JANE**), a palace guard
BERT (or **GERT**), a palace guard

THE PLACES

A CLEARING IN THE WOODS
NICK'S OFFICE
A PIRATE SHIP
RUMPLESTILTSKIN'S HOUSE
THE BEANSTALK
THE CASTLE

THE TIME

Whenever you're ready…

(A clearing in the woods with a large tree stump on one side. There is a large storybook sitting on the stump or leaning against it.)

(Enter **OLD GRANNY POSSUM,** *singing a little song. She looks around at the clearing for a moment and sighs with satisfaction. She crosses, picks up the book and sits on the stump. Another sigh of satisfaction – everything is just right.)*

(She opens the book, pages through it. After glancing at a few pages, She spots something wrong.)

GRANNY. What the heck…? I don't remember this story. Something's very wrong here.

(She looks at the cover of the book again.)

GRANNY. It's my storybook, all right.

(She pulls out a couple of loose pages, looks at them. On the back of each, there is a large "C" with a doodle of a crown above it.)

GRANNY. Well, no wonder. These aren't the regular pages. Someone's been fooling around with my book and stuck 'em in here. They better hope I don't catch them or bam zoom, to the moon, Alice! Oh, well, no harm done.

(She balls up the papers and tosses them into the audience, noticing them for the first time.)

GRANNY. *(to audience)* Here's a little souvenir for you. Wait a minute! Who the heck are you? And what're you doing in my woods? *(Waits for an answer – if none is forthcoming, have a plant do it.)* Came to see what? A play? Someone's pulling your leg, sweetie – there's no play here today. This is the woods. *(She speaks loudly and slowly as if talking to someone who is very dense.)* Woods! Trees! Bushes! Little birdies! No play. And if you think *I'm* going to tell you some fairy stories, you've got another think coming 'cause it's Old Granny Possum's day off so shoo!

(a pause)

GRANNY. Scat!

(a pause)

GRANNY. Scram!

(a pause)

GRANNY. Skee-daddle!

(a pause)

GRANNY. And yet you remain seated! Zut alors! If I tell you a story, one little story, mind you, do you promise to go away then? Cross your hearts and hope to die, stick a needle in your eye, crossies don't count? All right, then. One story. One! *(under her breath)* Can't even have a day off…bothering me…stupid story…

(**GRANNY** *opens the book, reads.*)

GRANNY. "Sleeping Beauty." Once upon a time, there was a girl named Beauty and she fell asleep and then a prince came by and woke her up and they lived happily ever after, the end.

(**GRANNY** *looks up hopefully.*)

GRANNY. There you go, perfectly nice story, thanks for coming. *(grumbles from audience)* What, not good enough for you? Fine. *(turns page)* "Cinderella." Once upon a time, there was a girl named Cinderella and a prince came by and gave her a glass slipper and they lived happily ever after, the end. Wasn't that nice? *(She waves goodbye.)* Good night and drive safely!

(**GRANNY** *looks expectantly at the audience, is disappointed that they are not buying it.*)

GRANNY. Still not enough? Jeez, you're awful picky, aren't you? Fine! "Snow White and the Seven Dwarves." Once upon a time, there was a beautiful but wicked queen named…

(*Enter* **QUEEN CUPCAKE**, *perhaps with a bit of crenellated wall to indicate that she is in a castle.*)

QUEEN CUPCAKE. Don't say it!

GRANNY. …Queen Cupcake!

QUEEN CUPCAKE. I told you not to say it!

(**GRANNY** *bursts out laughing.*)

GRANNY. Cupcake! That's a good one!

QUEEN CUPCAKE. You know, it's not very nice to laugh at someone's name. It's not like we get to pick our own names. And besides, somebody named Possum shouldn't be making fun of somebody named Cupcake, anyway!

GRANNY. She was very lovely to look at but rotten and evil on the inside, sort of like a delicious-looking chocolate pudding that you take a big bite out of and then discover it's full of worms! Her face was an angel's but her heart was a devil's. She was fair yet foul, beautiful yet abominable…

QUEEN CUPCAKE. (*having had enough*) Yes, yes, we get the point!

GRANNY. I just want to make sure that everyone appreciates the brilliant contrast between how you *look* and how you *act* because…

QUEEN CUPCAKE. I'm sure I speak for everyone when I say that we all understand your clever illustration of opposites combining to express the whole of man's intrinsically divided nature, yes? (*She looks to a member of the audience for their agreement.*) You get it, right? See? So can we please just move on?

GRANNY. Fine, you don't have to get all snotty about it. (*to the audience*) See what I mean? Anyway, she was used to being the best-looking gal in the kingdom and spent hours and hours sitting in front of her magic mirror.

(*Enter* **MAGIC MIRROR**. *The actor holds up an empty, ornate frame in front of his/her face and voila – a magic mirror! The* **MIRROR** *stands by the "castle."*)

QUEEN CUPCAKE. *(staring at mirror)* Mirror, mirror, on the wall, who's the fairest of them all?

MIRROR. *(in a "rapping" mode, busting a surprising move)*
Yo! I'm the Magic Mirror and I'm here to say,
I'm the magicest mirror in the land today!
Take a look in me,
And you will see,
Who the baddest maiden in the land must be!
Oh, Queenie, Queen, you know it's true,
That the freshest, fairest gal is you!
I cannot lie,
I will not try,
Of all the ladies, you are the most fly! Peace out!

(a pause)

QUEEN CUPCAKE. Beg pardon?

MIRROR. *(perhaps dancing a bit)* Bust a move, pretty Queenie! Let it out, sister!

QUEEN CUPCAKE. What?!

MIRROR. I'm just trying to inject a little hip-hop into the proceedings. You know, get down with the young people and the Daddy Mack and all that.

QUEEN CUPCAKE. Why don't you just do it the way you usually do it?

MIRROR. Homes of today ain't tripping with the way I "usually do it," boiy! Get with times, G! Word to your mama!

QUEEN CUPCAKE. Please don't bring my mama into this. This has nothing to do with my mama.

MIRROR. But...

QUEEN CUPCAKE. And it has nothing to do with my mama's butt, either. *(looking out at the audience)* Is there a magic mirror repairman in the house?

GRANNY. *(to **MIRROR**)* Look, lovey, is this really necessary? You're getting Cupcake all upset and you know how she gets when she's upset – throwing things and breaking things and shouting naughty words in a loud voice. No one likes an angry Cupcake, do they?

MIRROR. No.

GRANNY. Do it for me, then, there's a dear.

MIRROR. Fine. *(to* **QUEEN CUPCAKE***)* Go on. *(to* **GRANNY***)* For you.

QUEEN CUPCAKE. Mirror, mirror, on the wall, who's the fairest of them of all?

MIRROR. You know perfectly well.

QUEEN CUPCAKE. Who?!

MIRROR. You already know who!

QUEEN CUPCAKE. Say it! *(stamping her foot)*

MIRROR. You are, all right? You are, you are, you are! Satisfied?

QUEEN CUPCAKE. *(happily, with a sigh)* Poifectly!

GRANNY. The Queen was always the fairest of them all and so she was always very happy…

MIRROR. …because she had had her own way once again even though other people were only trying to make things better.

*(***MIRROR** *sticks out her tongue at* **QUEEN CUPCAKE** *who sticks her tongue out at* **MIRROR***.)*

GRANNY. Oh, that's a lovely example to set for impressionable children. Anywho, one day, Queen Cupcake married a King who had a lovely daughter named Snow White and unlike the evil, rotten Queen, this girl was as sweet and nice as she was beautiful.

(Enter **SNOW WHITE***. She is loudly "la-laing" a happy tune. Perhaps she flits through the audience, smiling and singing, or just makes a lap of the stage, flinging rose petals from a basket that she carries. Perhaps there is a bright light on her, perhaps we hear chirping birds or a chorus of voices heralding her arrival. At any rate, there is not doubt about it – she is a treasure.)*

(Finally, she stops.)

GRANNY. Finished?

*(***SNOW WHITE** *nods happily.)*

GRANNY. Sure?

(**SNOW WHITE** *nods happily again.*)

GRANNY. Because I don't want to proceed unless you're absolutely sure you're ready.

(**SNOW WHITE** *thinks, then nods happily again and throws a few petals affectionately at* **GRANNY**.)

GRANNY. The Queen suddenly had a rival for the title of most beautiful in the kingdom and, wouldn't you know it? It was her own step-daughter.

SNOW WHITE. *(curtsying and tossing a few petals)* Your Majesty.

QUEEN CUPCAKE. *(harumphing)* Harumph! Snow White – what kind of sissy name is that?

SNOW WHITE. One winter's day while she was sewing, my mother pricked her finger and the red, red blood fell on the white, white snow and she said…

QUEEN CUPCAKE. Yeah, yeah, yeah, I've heard the story. So I guess you think you're pretty easy on the eyes.

SNOW WHITE. Not half as much as you, step-mummy.

QUEEN CUPCAKE. And quite the little suck-up as well. Maybe you're not so bad after all.

GRANNY. The Queen tolerated the child until one day, the axe fell.

(**GRANNY** *laughs fiendishly. All look at her. She clears her throat, embarrassed.*)

QUEEN CUPCAKE. Mirror, mirror, on the wall, yadda yadda yadda.

MIRROR. Things have changed, oh Queenie, Queen,
You're just another old has-been.
I got some news
Give you the blues
This beauty pageant, you gonna lose.
See that new face? She is so fly!
You cannot beat her, don't even try!
Her spirit light,
She's so a-ight
Your own step-child, Princess Snow White!

SNOW WHITE. What a nice mirror.

QUEEN CUPCAKE. Yes, isn't it.

> (**QUEEN CUPCAKE** *crosses to* **MIRROR.**)

QUEEN CUPCAKE. *(all politeness)* May I?

> (**QUEEN CUPCAKE** *takes the frame, rips it to pieces, throws it on the stage and jumps on it. She picks up the pieces and hands them back to the* **MIRROR.**)

QUEEN CUPCAKE. Oopsy-daisy.

MIRROR. This isn't over, sister.

> (**MIRROR** *exits.*)

GRANNY. The Queen couldn't bear not being the best, talk about your type A personality, so she conceived a cunning plan.

QUEEN CUPCAKE. Really? *(thinking)* Cunning plan, cunning plan…hmmmm…drawing a bit of a blank here…

SNOW WHITE. *(trying to be helpful)* You could dip me in honey and tie me to an ant hill and let the ants eat me munch, munch, munch.

QUEEN CUPCAKE. Kind of a bigger project than I was planning on.

SNOW WHITE. You could put a paper bag of dog poop outside my door and light it on fire and then when I open the door and see the fire and stamp on it, I'd get poop all over my shoes, poop poop poop.

QUEEN CUPCAKE. Now, that I like but it doesn't really destroy your beauty which is the main thing I'm after.

SNOW WHITE. *(disappointed)* Oh.

QUEEN CUPCAKE. But don't get me wrong, I appreciate the help.

SNOW WHITE. What about if you let a tiger loose in my room and it chases me and mauls me and I'm screaming, "Help! Help! I'm being attacked by a tiger!" but no one comes to my aid because really, why would there be a tiger in my room?

QUEEN CUPCAKE. See? There you go! But – where would I get a tiger?

SNOW WHITE. Maybe the huntsman could find one in the deep, dark woods.

QUEEN CUPCAKE. The huntsman…hmmm…yes…I've got it! Run along, now, I want it to be a surprise.

SNOW WHITE. You're so thoughtful, step-mummy.

(SNOW WHITE *throws a few petals in* QUEEN CUP-CAKE*'s face and skips off.*)

QUEEN CUPCAKE. *(whistles)* Huntsman!

(*Enter* VINNIE. *He's from Brooklyn.*)

VINNIE. Yeah? What can I do for youse, Cupcake?

QUEEN CUPCAKE. That's Queen Cupcake to you. Vinnie, isn't it?

VINNIE. Yeah, but youse can call me Vinnie.

QUEEN CUPCAKE. Vinnie, I want youse…you to take Princess Snow White on a picnic in the woods.

VINNIE. A picnic? Me? Youse sure youse got youself the right guy?

QUEEN CUPCAKE. Oh, yes. Because once you're in there, I want you to… *(making a slashing motion across her throat)*

VINNIE. *(confused)* What?

QUEEN CUPCAKE. You know. *(She mimes stabbing him several times while shrieking the "Psycho" screams.)*

(VINNIE *shakes his head, still doesn't get it.*)

QUEEN CUPCAKE. You know!

(QUEEN CUPCAKE *throttles* VINNIE.)

VINNIE. Oh! Kill her.

QUEEN CUPCAKE. *(puts her hand over his mouth and looks around to see if anyone has overheard)* Shhh!!! Exactly. And then, and this is the good part, I want you to…

VINNIE. What are we having?

QUEEN CUPCAKE. Beg your pardon?

VINNIE. On the picnic. What are we having to eat?

QUEEN CUPCAKE. I don't know. That's not important because after you kill her, I want you to…

VINNIE. Deviled eggs?

QUEEN CUPCAKE. *(irritated)* Whatever.

VINNIE. And maybe sandwiches with the crusts cut off 'cause I don't like…

QUEEN CUPCAKE. *(more irritated)* Fine!

VINNIE. And maybe one of them cakes with pineapple chunks and walnuts and cream cheese frosting?

GRANNY. Hummingbird Cake?

VINNIE. Hummingbird Cake! I love Hummingbird Cake! And yet the baking of which is not an easy endeavor as one must resign one's self to a long stint in the kitchen when…

QUEEN CUPCAKE. *(extremely irritated)* You're missing the point! After you kill her, cut out her heart…

VINNIE. Well, that's not gonna improve my appetite any.

QUEEN CUPCAKE. … and bring it back to me so I know you did it!

VINNIE. *(hurt)* What, youse don't trust me? I'm a professional.

QUEEN CUPCAKE. It's not that. It's just that…oh, all right, I don't trust youse. Now go!

(**QUEEN CUPCAKE** *exits.*)

VINNIE. *(calling)* Princess Snow White!

(*Enter* **SNOW WHITE** *with a bit of her usual fanfare – a few petals, a few bars of music.*)

SNOW WHITE. Yes, Vinnie?

VINNIE. How would youse feel about a little picnic in the woods?

(**QUEEN CUPCAKE** *enters with a picnic basket and without stopping, crosses to* **VINNIE,** *hands it to him and exits again.*)

SNOW WHITE. Oh, I don't know. The woods are pretty scary.

QUEEN CUPCAKE. *(exiting)* There's Hummingbird Cake!

SNOW WHITE. I'm in!

> *(VINNIE and SNOW WHITE walk around the stage away from the "castle," perhaps through the audience, perhaps spreading petals on their merry way. Finally, they stop, take blanket out of basket, spread it out and sit on it.)*

SNOW WHITE. You seem sad, Vinnie. How can we turn that frown upside down?

VINNIE. Oh, Princess Snow White, alas is me. Queen Cupcake has ordered me to kill youse and bring back your heart.

SNOW WHITE. Ouch! Well, I wouldn't want you to get into any trouble on my account but I kind of need my heart.

VINNIE. Don't worry – youse smell like rosebuds and she smells like feet so my loyalty is definitely to youse.

SNOW WHITE. You're so sweet, Vinnie.

VINNIE. So what should we do? If I don't come back with a heart, you'll still be in danger and I'll be in trouble with my union – Huntsmen and Belly Dancers local 341.

SNOW WHITE. *(thinks)* Maybe you could you get a heart from the butcher shop. I'm sure they all look pretty much alike.

VINNIE. Youse come up with the best ideas, Princess. Phew! That's a load off my mind.

SNOW WHITE. You see? Problem solved! Now how about some of that cake and a smile?

> *(VINNIE smiles shyly and he and SNOW WHITE help themselves to cake from the basket.)*

GRANNY. So Vinnie and Snow White had their picnic and then he left her all alone in the deep, dark woods.

VINNIE. I'll be back to help youse in a little while. I gotta get a heart and show it to the Queen and then give it to my cat Mrs. Fluffington 'cause I've been away all day and she'll be mad. It might take a little while so don't youse go wandering off or youse could get into trouble.

SNOW WHITE. I'll just sit right here and listen to the birds sing and watch the sun shine on the flowers until you return.

VINNIE. Uh, okay, whatever turns youse on.

(VINNIE *takes picnic things and exits.*)

GRANNY. But Snow White grew bored listening to the birds and then it started to get dark and she began to get afraid.

SNOW WHITE. I'm beginning to get afraid.

GRANNY. She wandered through the trees looking for somewhere to spend the night.

SNOW WHITE. I must find somewhere to spend the night.

(SNOW WHITE *wanders about.*)

GRANNY. And at last she stumbled upon a little cottage in a clearing.

(*Opposite from the "castle," out comes a cottage pushed by a* STEVE *and* MERLE, *two dwarves.* SNOW WHITE *stumbles into it.*)

SNOW WHITE. Ooof! Look! A little cottage in a clearing!

GRANNY. It was the home of the seven dwarves.

(GRANNY *looks at them, disapproves of their size.*)

STEVE. We're tall for our height.

(STEVE *is the brighter of the two.* MERLE *is bigger and a bit dense.*)

MERLE. *(in his low, deep voice)* And we prefer to be called "little people."

STEVE. *(nervously)* Wait. Are you sure it's seven?

GRANNY. *(checking book)* It *is* called "Snow White And The S*even* Dwarves."

MERLE. Seven *Little People.*

STEVE. That's funny because I haven't actually seen any others around here except for Merle and me.

MERLE. *(counting on his fingers)* How many is seven, Steve?

STEVE. The Brady Bunch minus Jan and Alice.

MERLE. What?

STEVE. Two sets of Jonas Brothers and a Miley Cyrus. *(or whoever)*

MERLE. Kevin is so dreamy!

STEVE. *(to **GRANNY**)* Does it have to be seven? I mean, is it intrinsic to the plot that there really be seven actual dwarves?

MERLE. Although Joe is pretty dreamy, too…

STEVE. Not now, Merle.

GRANNY. Seven is the accepted number.

STEVE. But it wouldn't really ruin the story or anything if there weren't seven, would it?

GRANNY. So this is now the story of "Snow White And Just The Two Very Tall Dwarves?"

MERLE. Little people!

STEVE. Rolls off the tongue, don't it?

GRANNY. Fine, fine. I just want to get through it so these people will go away! Snow White stumbled onto the cottage of the two…

MERLE & GRANNY. …little people.

STEVE. Hello. Who are you?

SNOW WHITE. I'm Princess Snow White. Who are you?

STEVE. I'm Steve.

MERLE. And I'm Steve.

STEVE. I'm Steve. You're Merle. What are you doing in these deep, dark woods?

MERLE. I live here with you, remember?

STEVE. *(to **MERLE**)* Not you! Her.

SNOW WHITE. I'm lost.

STEVE. Not anymore! You can stay here with us.

SNOW WHITE. That's very kind but I'm afraid it might put you in danger. My stepmother Queen Cupcake wants me dead.

STEVE. Never fear. We'll protect you.

MERLE. If any cupcakes come after you, we'll just eat 'em right up!

STEVE. Don't mind Merle. He's harmless.

MERLE. *(looking around)* Come on out, you old cupcakes! I dare you to try something! I'll eat you up with one hand tied behind my back!

STEVE. Confused…but harmless.

GRANNY. So Snow White stayed with Steve and Merle. They played…

(They play patty-cake.)

GRANNY. They sang…

SNOW WHITE, STEVE, MERLE. *(singing)* "On top of spaghetti, all covered with cheese,

I lost my poor meatball when somebody sneezed."

GRANNY. They got down and boogied the night away…

SNOW WHITE, STEVE, MERLE. *(singing as they boogie)* "It rolled off the table and onto the floor,

And then my poor meatball, rolled out of the door."

*(**SNOW WHITE, STEVE** and **MERLE** exit while boogie-ing.)*

*(Enter **QUEEN CUPCAKE** and **VINNIE** opposite at the castle.)*

GRANNY. Meanwhile…

MERLE. *(singing off)* "It rolled in the garden…"

STEVE. *(off)* Not now, Merle!

GRANNY. Meanwhile, Queen Cupcake had been fooled by Vinnie and believed Snow White to be dead.

VINNIE. *(holding out a heart)* Here is her heart, your royal Cupcakedness.

QUEEN CUPCAKE. At last! I'm the most beautiful again! Well, bleah, don't just stand there with that thing, what do you think I'm going to do with it? Take it away!

VINNIE. *(calling)* Mrs. Fluffington! Here, kitty! Look what I got for youse!

*(***VINNIE*** exits. There is a loud "meow" off.)*

GRANNY. So you can understand that Cupcake got a nasty shock when she looked in her mirror a few days later.

*(***MIRROR*** enters. The "frame" is good as new.)*

MIRROR. *(with a little wave)* Remember me?

QUEEN CUPCAKE. But I smashed you!

MIRROR. Hello! *Magic* mirror. You really believe a simple smashing is going to get rid of me? I don't think so.

QUEEN CUPCAKE. Fine. Mirror, mirror, blah, blah, blah.

MIRROR. Oh, Queenie, Queen, the news is bad.

I'm going to make you oh so sad.

I know you think Snow White is gone

But you are, you are, you are wrong!

Contrary to what you believe,

She's still alive – don't be naive.

She's living with two tiny men

Out in the forest, down in the glen,*

And still so much more fair than you

So let it out – boo hoo hoo hoo!

For beauty is not just your face,

It's the good in your heart, a state of grace.

And you will never be the best

'cause you are meaner than all the rest!

Can't touch this!

QUEEN CUPCAKE. *(to ***GRANNY***)* I hate that mirror. *(throwing a tantrum)* What?! Snow White still alive?! I don't believe this! *(She stops abruptly.)* Interesting. I know of only two tiny men in our forest – Steve and Merle. Hmmm. I suppose I must now come up with yet another cunning

*See Author's Note on Page 60.

plan to do away with Snow White once and for all. *(thinks)* And I got nothing. If only Snow White were here – she's so good with cunning plans.

GRANNY. *(impatiently)* We'll never get through this if you keep taking so long! Just dip an apple in some poison and get her to take a bite. Sheesh!

QUEEN CUPCAKE. Poisoned apple, you say? Perfect! What a twisted little mind you have! I'll disguise myself as an old hag, trick the little twit into eating the poisoned apple and viola! *(imitating Porky Pig)* The-the-the-the-that's all, folks!

(**QUEEN CUPCAKE** *exits.*)

GRANNY. So, the Queen made herself look ugly…

MIRROR. *(exiting)*…which wasn't very hard to do…

QUEEN CUPCAKE. *(off)* I heard that!

GRANNY. …whipped up a poisoned apple and set out for the forest. Meanwhile, Snow White and her new dwarf friends had been enjoying themselves, doing whatever it is dwarves do to have fun.

(*Enter* **SNOW WHITE, STEVE** *and* **MERLE**.)

STEVE. *(shuffling or fanning a deck of cards)* …and you keep raising until somebody calls. Do you have any money of your own?

GRANNY. But the day came when Steve and Merle had to go back to work.

STEVE. Don't worry, we'll be back soon. Just remember what we taught you – don't go out into the forest…

MERLE. …don't talk to strangers…

SNOW WHITE. …and never draw to an inside straight. I'll remember.

(**STEVE** *and* **MERLE** *exit.*)

GRANNY. While she was alone, the Queen came by to get rid of her once and for all.

(*Enter* **QUEEN CUPCAKE**, *disguised as a hag and carrying a basket of apples. She crosses by the cottage, limping and out of breath.*)

SNOW WHITE. Hello, old hag! Do you need some help?

QUEEN CUPCAKE. Oh, yes, I'm so tired and thirsty and I have a big blister on my toe. If only I could rest a moment and get a drink of water…

SNOW WHITE. Please let me…

QUEEN CUPCAKE. Go away! I'm not supposed to talk to strangers!

SNOW WHITE. But I'm not a stranger. My name is Snow White. What's yours?

QUEEN CUPCAKE. My name is…uh, um…Mrs… *(sees her apples)* …Apple…basket…

SNOW WHITE. Pleased to meet you, Mrs. Applebasket. There now, you see? Now we aren't strangers anymore so you must let me get you a drink of water.

(SNOW WHITE gets a glass from the cottage and gives it to QUEEN CUPCAKE.)

QUEEN CUPCAKE. Aren't you sweet? For being so nice, let me give you one of my tasty apples.

(QUEEN CUPCAKE gives SNOW WHITE a beautiful red apple.)

QUEEN CUPCAKE. No, wait, wrong one.

(QUEEN CUPCAKE takes it back and gives SNOW WHITE another red apple.)

QUEEN CUPCAKE. Uh, that's not it, either. *(sighs)* I just had it here a minute ago…

(QUEEN CUPCAKE roots around in basket until she finds a black and rotten apple, perhaps in reality a plum or prune.)

QUEEN CUPCAKE. There we go! Doesn't that look delicious?

(SNOW WHITE dubiously takes the apple.)

SNOW WHITE. Yummy. I'll…save it for after dinner.

QUEEN CUPCAKE. No! It might…go bad. Eat it now while it's still fresh.

SNOW WHITE. But…

QUEEN CUPCAKE. Eat it!

> (**SNOW WHITE** *takes a bite.*)

QUEEN CUPCAKE. How does it taste?

SNOW WHITE. *(making a terrible face but trying to be nice)* It's… well, it's…arg!

> (**SNOW WHITE** *falls down dead.*)

QUEEN CUPCAKE. Perfect! And yet I suppose she could be faking, the little beast. *(calling)* Oh, Mirror?

> (**MIRROR** *enters*)

MIRROR. Snow White is dead, you win this round.
She'll soon be in the cold, cold ground.
You may be fairest, you may be rich,
But you are still an evil…

QUEEN CUPCAKE. Hey hey!

MIRROR. …witch.

> (**MIRROR** *and* **QUEEN CUPCAKE** *exit.*)

GRANNY. So, Snow White was dead, Queen Cupcake was happy and Steve and Merle were sad beyond belief.

> (**QUEEN CUPCAKE** *exits.* **STEVE** *and* **MERLE** *enter. They see* **SNOW WHITE** *and drop down next to her, crying.*)

STEVE. Snow White! What's happened? *(He picks up her hand, lets it fall.)* She's dead!

MERLE. Did the cupcakes get her?

STEVE. I guess they did.

MERLE. *(shaking his fist)* Curse you, evil cupcakes! How can something so delicious and covered in sprinkles be so bad? Oh, I cannot bear to lose her. Let us keep her here with us so we might look upon her beauty forever.

STEVE. *(with a face)* What happens when she starts to rot?

MERLE. *(shaking his fist at* **STEVE***)* Look upon her beauty forever!

GRANNY. And then, one day, Prince Charming came riding by and spotted her.

(*Enter* **PRINCE CHARMING** *riding a hobby horse.*)

PRINCE. Who is that lovely creature?

STEVE. It is Snow White, your Majesty.

MERLE. We believe she is under an evil spell for she neither breathes nor moves and yet she remains as beautiful as if she were still alive.

STEVE. And thank goodness for that because if she started to smell, we'd have to throw her out.

MERLE. Never!

PRINCE. I must kiss such a wondrous girl.

MERLE. Wait! She's been like this for a while. You don't want to chance it.

(**MERLE** *takes out a breath spritzer, opens* **SNOW WHITE**'s *mouth and "spritzes" it. Then he spritzes under his armpits for good measure.*)

MERLE. Okay, try it now.

(**PRINCE** *kisses* **SNOW WHITE**.)

PRINCE. Mmm, minty!

GRANNY. And then, guess what happened? The piece of poisoned apple that was stuck in her mouth fell out and she woke up. Isn't that nice?

(**SNOW WHITE** *wakes up and spits out the piece of apple at the* **PRINCE**.)

SNOW WHITE. Ptooee! What happened?

PRINCE. You were under an evil spell but I broke it with a kiss.

SNOW. I love you! Marry me!

PRINCE. (*to audience*) What a refreshingly modern girl.

STEVE. I'll bet Queen Cupcake is behind all this. Let us hunt her down and kill her!

PRINCE. What strange, blood-thirsty dwarves.

MERLE. (*proudly*) Blood-thirsty little people.

GRANNY. So they all went to the castle where Queen Cupcake's rottenness was revealed.

(STEVE, MERLE, SNOW WHITE and the PRINCE cross to the castle.)

STEVE, SNOW WHITE, PRINCE. Send out the evil Queen!

MERLE. And all her evil cupcakes!

(Enter QUEEN in her disguise and MIRROR.)

QUEEN CUPCAKE. Who? The Queen? Oh, I'm afraid she left a few days ago. Something about retiring to Miami Beach…

SNOW WHITE. That's her! That's the Queen in disguise!

MERLE. Let me at her, let me at her! I got me a hankering for something sweet!

STEVE. *(holding MERLE back)* Easy, Merle! That cupcake is pure evil.

PRINCE. *(to QUEEN CUPCAKE)* You are a wicked woman and I banish you forever!

GRANNY. Finally – the end! And they all lived…

STEVE. Shh! It isn't over yet.

MIRROR. Ha ha! You're banished!

QUEEN CUPCAKE. Big whoop! I'll just go to another kingdom and be the most beautiful woman there!

(During the following, BLUEBEARD and a band of scurvy PIRATES quietly enter, possibly through the audience. BLUEBEARD hands a note to someone in the audience while PIRATES sneak up on GRANNY, gently gag her, pick her up in her sitting position and carry her off. Her book falls to the ground unnoticed.)

MIRROR. Not so fast!
The life you've known is over now,
So get a grip, don't have a cow.
Now that your spell has been reversed,
It's you I say has now been cursed!
That ugly look fixed on your face
Will not come off – it's stuck in place!
So look in me, if you but dare,
Never again will you be fair!
Word!

(**QUEEN CUPCAKE** *clutches her face and cries out in anguish.*)

QUEEN CUPCAKE. My face! My beautiful face! What have you done?!

MIRROR. They don't call me a magic mirror for nothing, sweetheart.

MERLE. Huzzah! Good guys one, cupcakes nothing!

STEVE. Justice, sweet justice!

QUEEN CUPCAKE. My face! Change it back, do you hear me, change it back or I'll…I'll…

(**QUEEN CUPCAKE** *dissolves into a heap of sorrow.*)

STEVE. You'll what? You've got no more cunning plans, isn't that right, Granny Possum. (*He looks around.*) Granny Possum?

MERLE. (*looking around*) Hey, where'd she go? Did the cupcakes get her, too?

PRINCE CHARMING. Isn't she supposed to say "…and they all lived happily ever after?"

SNOW WHITE. She always says "…and they all lived happily ever after."

(**PRINCE CHARMING, SNOW WHITE, STEVE, MERLE** *and* **MIRROR** *all look around for*)

STEVE, MERLE, MIRROR, SNOW WHITE, PRINCE CHARMING. Granny Possum? Granny Possum!

(**SNOW WHITE, PRINCE CHARMING, STEVE, MERLE** *and* **MIRROR** *exit, still looking and calling for* **GRANNY**.)

(*blackout*)

(**QUEEN CUPCAKE** *exits taking the "castle" with her.*)

(*Bluesy jazz music plays, mostly horn. This is Nick's theme. A single spot shines on the stump area. Enter* **NICK TICKLE**. *He is dressed in a suit, trench coat and fedora. He sucks a lollypop and pushes a desk. He positions the desk in the light in front of the stump, leans back on the desk and speaks to the audience.*)

NICK. I've got a fairy tale for you. Once upon a time, there was a guy, just an average guy, just an average regular Joe. And then one day, some dame broke his heart by running away with his best friend and they took the poor slob's innocence along with his bank account. The end. How do you like that story? Not very happy, is it. I'm sure glad it didn't happen to me! Things have been pretty good here at the office ever since I broke the Goldilocks case wide open. Lots of new clients, lots of pretty gals. If you live in Fairy Tale Land and you got a problem no one else can solve, there's only one person to turn to and you're looking at him. I don't carry a gun. I use my brains. I'm Nick Tickle. I'm a detective.

(**NICK** *sits on the stump behind the desk.*)

(*Enter* **STEVE** *and* **MERLE.**)

STEVE. Are you Nick Tickle, the detective?

NICK. Have you heard a word I said?

STEVE. We heard your ad on the radio and we want to hire you.

STEVE & MERLE. *(singing to the tune of "Row, Row, Row Your Boat")*
"Tickle, Tickle, he's the one,
He's the one for you!
In a pickle, call on Tickle,
He's the one for you! Hey!"

MERLE. I like to sing it over and over again! *(sings)* "Tickle, Tickle, he's the one…"

STEVE. Not now, Merle.

NICK. Yeah, I'm Tickle. What'd you want, Bub?

STEVE. It's Steve, actually.

MERLE. And I'm Steve.

STEVE. And this is Merle. We need your help.

NICK. So go talk to the Boy Scouts.

STEVE. We need somebody a little tougher.

NICK. So go talk to the *Girl* Scouts.

STEVE. The Gingerbread Man said you're the one can clean up the mess after the cookie crumbles.

NICK. And I put Humpty Dumpty back together again after somebody pushed him. So what's your point?

MERLE. *(horrified)* Humpty Dumpty was pushed?!

STEVE. You gotta rescue Granny Possum!

NICK. That nice old broad that tells the stories?

MERLE. Somebody kidnapped her! *(looks around suspiciously and in a loud whisper)* It might've been cupcakes.

NICK. Cupcakes?

STEVE. He means Queen Cupcake but it couldn't've been her – we were with her when it happened. Anyway, we figure if anybody can get her back, you can. *(He pulls out a pouch and hands it to* **NICK.***)* For your fee. Everybody gave what they could. Except me. I'm a little short. Get it? I'm a dwarf and I'm a little short? *(to audience)* Oh, come on, that's funny.

NICK. *(opening pouch and examining some coins)* How do you know she was snatched?

STEVE. One minute she was there telling a story…

MERLE. …our story!

STEVE. …and the next she was gone.

NICK. Maybe she just wandered off. Maybe she got tired of telling stories.

STEVE. She would never get tired of telling stories! She's very dedicated.

MERLE. *(sadly)* And she never even got to say "…and they all lived happily ever after."

NICK. That's not much proof of kidnapping.

STEVE. Look, if she did just wander away, it shouldn't be hard to find her so this'll be easy money for you. Won't you take the case?

NICK. Of course I'll take the case. Who said I wouldn't take the case? I'm on the case even as we speak. So where and when did this supposed abduction take place?

STEVE. Just a little while ago. She was sitting on that stump in her favorite clearing in the forest...

MERLE. ...and when we looked around, she was gone!

NICK. So I guess that stump is the place to start. Thanks for the case, boys, I'll be in touch. And don't worry. You did the right thing coming to me. I'll find Granny Possum or my name isn't Nick Tickle.

MERLE. *(singing)* "Tickle, Tickle, he's the one, He's the one for you!"

STEVE. Not now, Merle. Come on, I'll buy you a cupcake.

MERLE. Ahhhh! No evil cupcakes!

(**STEVE** *and* **MERLE** *exit.*)

NICK. *(to audience)* Well, what do you think about that? Sounds like it's going to be a pretty tough case. Kindly old grandmother snatched in broad daylight, right in front of witnesses, no less. Whoever did it is pretty dangerous. I could use somebody watching my back. Say, I don't suppose you folks would like to help me? Great! Raise your right hand...your other right hand...and repeat after me: I...your name...no, I mean say your name...oh very funny...do solemnly swear to help Nick Tickle...crack "The Case of the Missing Granny." Now blow a raspberry to make it official. *(He blows a raspberry.)* Excellent! You have now all been deputized as Junior Detectives. I'm counting on you so pay close attention. We can't afford to let any clues slip by us. Granny Possum's very life may be in our hands. I'll meet you at the clearing in the woods.

*(Lights out on **NICK** as he exits, pushing his desk out ahead of him.)*

*(Lights up on the far side of the clearing. Enter **PRINCE CHARMING** with horse.)*

PRINCE. *(to audience)* Hello there! Remember me? Prince Charming? I was just wondering who was going to be telling the stories now that Granny Possum is gone. Thought I might volunteer to help out.

(**PRINCE** *crosses to stump, picks up book, leafs through it.*)

PRINCE. Let's see. Same old, same old…say, maybe you'd like to hear *my* story for a change? Once upon a time there was a prince…

(*Enter* **NICK.**)

NICK. *(to audience)* Good, you found it. The scene of the crime is always the best place to begin so…

(**NICK** *notices* **PRINCE CHARMING.**)

NICK. Oh! Hey there. Say, aren't you…

PRINCE. Charming. Prince Charming.

(*They shake hands.*)

NICK. That's right. We met at Cinderella's ball that time.

PRINCE. And you're…

NICK. Nick Tickle…

PRINCE. The detective!

NICK. Guilty as charged.

PRINCE. What are you doing here?

NICK. I'm investigating Granny Possum's disappearance and I understand this was the last place she was seen.

PRINCE. We were just finishing up and when we turned around, she was gone.

NICK. What're you doing here?

PRINCE. *(holding up the book)* Thought I might take over until she gets back. You know, read to the kiddies and keep things going.

NICK. That's good of you.

PRINCE. I do what I can. Well, I'll get out of your way. Let me know if I can do anything to help. We all want Granny back safe and sound.

NICK. We sure do. See you later.

(**PRINCE** *exits with storybook and horse.*)

(*looking around*) I can't believe nobody saw anything. And kidnappers always leave a ransom note.

(Hopefully, someone in the audience will speak up. Or have a plant do it.)

NICK. You saw something? What did you see? Pirates? What did they do? How many were there? *(etc.)* That sounds like Bluebeard's men. Can I see the note?

*(**NICK** gets the note from the audience. On the back there may be seen a large "C" with a doodle of a crown above it.)*

NICK. *(reading note)* "I've got Granny Possum. If you want to see her again, leave 20 golden eggs in a basket by the beanstalk and she will be released unharmed." And there's some kind of mark here on the back. Great. Where are we going to find a hen that lays golden eggs? *(waits for answer)* The giant on top of the beanstalk? Say, that's right. But he would never give us any of his golden eggs. We're going to have to get Granny back on our own. Where do you think we should start, partners? Who should we talk to first? *(waits for answer)* The pirates? That's a great idea. You're pretty smart. I'm glad you're helping me out. I'll meet you at their ship!

(If an intermission is desired, take it now.)

*(**NICK** starts to exit.)*

NICK. Wait a minute! I'm a little worried about talking to Bluebeard all alone. I need somebody to watch out for me. Is there anyone out there who's brave enough to come up here and help me?

*(**NICK** chooses a volunteer from the audience to come up on stage.)*

NICK. What's your name? Okay, *(name)*, you're with me. *(to audience)* You know where Bluebeard's ship "The Bloody Queen" is docked, don't you? I'll see you there.

*(**NICK** exits with volunteer. Off, the volunteer should be given a wooden sword and told to enter and press the sword gently into **BLUEBEARD**'s back when **NICK** gives the signal.)*

*(Meanwhile, enter **BLUEBEARD** and his pirate gang. They bring on the "ship" and are drinking mugs of root beer.)*

BLUEBEARD. *(who speaks in a typical pirate English accent)* Sixteen men on a dead man's chest, yo-ho-ho and a bottle of root beer! *(flourishing his mug)* Drink up, me hearties, yo ho! We've had a good day's work, haven't we, lads!

PIRATES. Huzzah!

BLUEBEARD. I've never seen a kidnapping go so smooth-like. Now how's about we have a little contest to see who can make me laugh so hard that root beer comes out me nose? A gold coin to the winner!

PIRATES. Huzzah!

*(**PIRATES** begin trying to make **BLUEBEARD** laugh.)*

*(Meanwhile, **NICK** enters, unnoticed by the **PIRATES**. He makes an "OK" sign to the audience and approaches the **PIRATES**.)*

NICK. Ahoy, Captain Bluebeard. Permission to come aboard.

BLUEBEARD. Permission granted.

*(**NICK** "comes aboard.")*

BLUEBEARD. And what scabrous landlubber dares come see me, the King of the Pirates, the most dreaded buccaneer on all the Spanish Main? Shiver me timbers and pluck out me eyes if it isn't Nick Pickle.

NICK. Tickle.

BLUEBEARD. Beg your pardon, Pickle? I didn't quite catch that.

NICK. It's Tickle!

BLUEBEARD. What?

NICK. Tickle! Tickle, Tickle, Tickle!

BLUEBEARD. You heard him, men!

*(**PIRATES** run over and tickle **NICK**.)*

NICK. All right, enough! It's all fun and games until somebody loses an eye!

PIRATE WITH EYE PATCH. You can say that again!

NICK. Captain, I'd like to ask you a few questions.

BLUEBEARD. What's in it for me?

(**NICK** *takes out a coin and flips it over to* **BLUEBEARD**.)

NICK. How about a piece of silver?

(**BLUEBEARD** *bites on the coin and puts it in his pocket.*)

BLUEBEARD. Ask away.

NICK. Where were you and your men earlier this afternoon?

BLUEBEARD. We've been here on The Bloody Queen all day. The tide's against us so we've not been able to weigh anchor and set sail.

NICK. Didn't go ashore for maybe a bit of…oh, I don't know…kidnapping?

BLUEBEARD. *(the picture of innocence)* Mr. Tickle, do we look like a bunch of kidnappers to you?

NICK. As a matter of fact, you do.

BLUEBEARD. Blast! If you're talking about Granny Possum, I don't believe you can pin her disappearance on us.

NICK. *(indicating audience)* As a matter of fact, there are witnesses who saw you snatch her.

BLUEBEARD. Double blast! Well, suppose we did. It's not like kidnapping's against the law or anything.

NICK. As a matter of fact, it is.

BLUEBEARD. Triple blast! Hold on – where are me manners? Would you like a root beer, Mr. Tickle? Talking's thirsty work. A mug of our special root beer for Mr. Tickle!

(**BLUEBEARD** *signals to a* **PIRATE** *who hands a mug to* **NICK** *who drinks.*)

NICK. Thanks, that's very kind of you.

BLUEBEARD. Have you ever heard the story of how me late wife got into trouble by poking her nose into something that didn't concern her?

NICK. I don't believe I have.

BLUEBEARD. I told her not to look in a certain room and she went ahead and looked anyway. Things didn't turn out so well for her in the end. She got so upset by what she saw that she…*(makes slash across his throat)* …lost her head.

NICK. That's a nice story but what's it got to do with me?

BLUEBEARD. Just fair warning that maybe this kidnapping ain't any of your business and you could get into trouble poking your nose in it. I'm sure you like your head just where it is.

NICK. I appreciate your concern, Captain, but as I've been hired to find Granny Possum, it is my business.

BLUEBEARD. Well, that's a shame because I meself have been hired to keep Granny Possum from being found. Boyos?

(**BLUEBEARD** *gives a signal and the* **PIRATES** *rush over and grab* **NICK.**)

BLUEBEARD. This has been a very pleasant conversation, Mr. Tickle, but I believe the time has come for you to leave my ship…

NICK. With pleasure!

BLUEBEARD. …by walking the plank!

(*cheers from the* **PIRATES**)

NICK. I'm afraid I must decline your kind offer, Captain.

BLUEBEARD. Oh, I'm not asking you, Mr. Tickle. I'm telling you.

(*The* **PIRATES** *bring* **NICK** *over to the "plank."*)

(**NICK** *gives his signal. The audience volunteer should now enter behind* **BLUEBEARD** *and stick the sword in his back.*)

NICK. Not so fast, Bluebeard! My partner is ready to run you through if you don't let me go.

BLUEBEARD. *(reacting to a "poke" by the sword)* Ouch! Got the drop on me, have you, Tickle? Very clever. Anyone ever tell you you'd make a fine pirate? Let him go, lads!

(The **PIRATES** *release* **NICK.***)*

BLUEBEARD. Blast and damn your quick wits, Nick Tickle!

NICK. If you want to keep out of the hangman's noose, you'll tell me where Granny Possum is.

BLUEBEARD. *(rubbing his neck)* I can't tell you that.

*(***NICK*** makes a sign and the volunteer pokes* **BLUE-BEARD** *again.)*

BLUEBEARD. I can't tell you because I don't know! I found a shiny gold coin and this note in me cabin this very morning.

*(***BLUEBEARD*** hands* **NICK** *a note from his pocket. The same "C" mark can be seen on the back.)*

NICK. *(reading)* "This is down payment on the kidnapping of Granny Possum. You'll receive twenty more coins when you deliver her unharmed to the beanstalk today." And there's that mark on the back again.

BLUEBEARD. It was a simple operation. We grabbed her easy as you please, tied her up and took her to the beanstalk. There was a pretty pile of gold coins waiting for us, not a scratch on 'em. We scooped 'em up and left her there and that's all I know. Now will you kindly ask your partner to stop poking me in the bum with that sword!

NICK. I appreciate your hospitality, Captain. Good job, *(volunteer's name)*. We got what we came for. Let's go.

*(***NICK*** and volunteer exit.)*

*(***PIRATES*** begin to exit with their "ship.")*

BLUEBEARD. *(calling out after)* Think you've pulled as fast one on me, have you, Tickle? You'd best sail a true course and keep a watchful eye out for me Jolly Roger.

(He indicates his pirate flag.) I've got a funny feeling that we're going to meet again and this time, *(He flourishes his sword.)* …I'll let me blade do the talking!

(BLUEBEARD and PIRATES laugh and exit with ship.)

(Enter NICK and volunteer.)

NICK. *(to volunteer)* Thanks, *(name)*. I would've been in real trouble there without your help. *(to audience)* Let's have a big hand for *(name)* the Brave!

(NICK sends volunteer back to their seat.)

NICK. *(a trifle unsteady)* So somebody is willing to spend a lot of gold to get Granny out of the picture. But why? It can't be for the ransom – whoever hired Bluebeard has plenty of gold already. Is it me or is this forest spinning? I don't think I should've had that root beer…

(Perhaps some effects to indicate NICK's predicament – swirling lights, whirling music/sounds, BLUEBEARD's voice laughing.)

(In this crazy cacophony, PUSS IN BOOTS enters unseen and hides herself behind the stump.)

(NICK collapses, unconscious.)

(Lights and sound back to normal.)

(Enter BLUEBEARD. He creeps up on NICK, sword in hand, clearly planning mischief.)

BLUEBEARD. Now, Mr. Tickle, we'll see who's more clever – the pirate or the detective!

PUSS. I wouldn't do that if I were you.

BLUEBEARD. *(spinning around)* Who's there?

PUSS. Someone more talented with a sword than you, mutinous dog.

BLUEBEARD. So prove it! Come out and face me if you dare!

(PUSS pokes out her head, a harmless cat.)

PUSS. Meow!

BLUEBEARD. Oh, sending out a harmless pussy cat to meet me challenge? What kind of fighter hides behind a fluffy kitty?

(**BLUEBEARD** *strides around, looking for his challenger. When his back is to* **PUSS**, *she stands up, whips out her sword.*)

PUSS. *(tapping* **BLUEBEARD** *on the shoulder with her sword)* What kind of fighter takes advantage of an unconscious opponent?

BLUEBEARD. *(spinning around)* Why, a dirty fighter, of course – a pirate!

(*There is a great duel. At some point, a gold coin falls from* **BLUEBEARD**'s *pocket.*)

(*Finally,* **PUSS** *gets the advantage.*)

PUSS. Run back to your ship, you poxy privateer. I allow you live only so that you might tell others how you were bested by...Puss In Boots!

(*As* **BLUEBEARD** *turns to run off, she slaps his butt with her sword.* **BLUEBEARD** *exits.*)

(**PUSS** *crosses to* **NICK** *and slaps him awake.*)

NICK. *(drowsily)*...can't go to school today, Mom, I have a stomach ache...

PUSS. Wake up and thank me for saving your life, fish bait.

NICK. *(regaining his senses)* Hmmph? Saving my life?

PUSS. Captain Bluebeard was about to make fishkabobs out of you but I persuaded him otherwise.

NICK. Why?

PUSS. I can't stand the sight of blood.

NICK. Who are you?

PUSS. Who do you think?

NICK. The Cat in the Hat?

PUSS. Puss In Boots, fish bait! Who are you and why is Bluebeard after your skin?

NICK. I'm Nick Tickle. I'm working on the Granny Possum kidnapping case and Bluebeard's up to his salty elbows in it.

PUSS. And I let him get away!

(**PUSS** *starts to exit.*)

NICK. Wait! I've already found out everything he knows. He was hired to kidnap Granny but he doesn't know who hired him. Why do you care?

PUSS. You're not the only one trying to find her. I came here as soon as I heard. A criminal always returns to the scene of the crime. I was sure whoever took her would come back here again.

NICK. Have you seen anyone?

PUSS. Just you and Bluebeard. Does he still have her?

NICK. No, he left her by the beanstalk.

(**NICK** *sits on the stump.* **PUSS** *begins searching the ground.*)

NICK. *(to audience)* Well, I'm stumped. Get it? Oh, come on, that's funny. *(to* **PUSS***)* What're you looking for?

PUSS. When I was fighting that bilge rat, something fell out of his coat.

(**PUSS** *finds the coin.*)

PUSS. And here it is!

(**PUSS** *hands coin to* **NICK.***)*

NICK. It's a gold coin. *(to audience)* Partners, what did Captain Bluebeard tell us about how he'd been paid? *(waits for an answer about beautiful gold coins)* Exactly! Beautiful gold coins! This must be one of them.

PUSS. Can it tell us anything useful?

NICK. We need an expert. *(to audience)* Who do you think might be able to tell us about gold? Who knows all about gold because he can spin straw into it? *(waits for the answer "Rumplestiltskin")* Yes, that funny little man Rumplestiltskin! I think we should show him this coin and see what he says.

PUSS. Mind if I tag along?

NICK. After tangling with Bluebeard, anybody handy with a sword is a friend of mine. Come on. *(to audience)* We'll meet you at Rumplestiltskin's house.

(**NICK** *and* **PUSS** *exit.*)

(*Enter* **MRS. STILTSKIN** *pushing on her house. She sweeps in front of it with a broom.*)

MRS. STILTSKIN. All I can say is, he better have a baby in his arms when he comes home or he can start spinning straw into another wife…

(*Enter* **RUMPLESTILTSKIN**. *He crosses to her fearfully.*)

MRS. STILTSKIN. So where's the baby you promised me?

RUMPLESTILTSKIN. I didn't get it.

MRS. STILTSKIN. (*hitting him with her broom*) So I noticed! Why not?

RUMPLESTILTSKIN. The same old thing…

MRS. STILTSKIN. Again?! Why can't you just shut up for once about giving them a second chance?!

RUMPLESTILTSKIN. I can't help it! Whenever I spin some woman's straw into gold and demand her baby in return, she brings up letting her off the hook if she can guess my name.

MRS. STILTSKIN. Guessing your name – what a stupid idea!

RUMPLESTILTSKIN. I know, I know! That first girl I helped, that miller's daughter, what a blabbermouth! She must have told the entire kingdom! Now everyone wants the same deal. And they all seem to know my name!

MRS. STILTSKIN. Look, it's simple. I want a baby. I need a baby! I gotta have a baby!!!

RUMPLESTILTSKIN. Well, I don't know what else I can do.

MRS. STILTSKIN. (*She takes a vial from a pocket in her apron.*) Fortunately, someone in this marriage has a brain. While you were away, I went to see the witch who lives in the candy house and she gave me…

RUMPLESTILTSKIN. Candy for dinner?

MRS. STILTSKIN. …this magic amnesia potion. Whoever drinks it will forget everything they know so all you have to do is get the next woman to drink it before she starts guessing and that baby's as good as mine!

RUMPLESTILTSKIN. Wife, that is an excellent idea! But how do I restore her memory after?

MRS. STILTSKIN. You simply say,
"Boogey boogey boogey boo
Take that magic off of you!"
and she'll be right as rain.

RUMPLESTILTSKIN. What was that again?

MRS. STILTSKIN. "Boogey boogey boogey boo
Take that magic off of you!"

RUMPLESTILTSKIN. You are so much more clever than I.

(RUMPLESTILTSKIN *puts up his hand.*)

MRS. STILTSKIN. (*slapping him a "high five"*) And don't you forget it.

(*Enter* NICK *and* PUSS.)

NICK. (*to audience*) Good, you found the place okay. (*to* PUSS) Rumplestiltskin knows all about gold. He'll be able to tell us what we need to know.

PUSS. How are you going to get him to help?

NICK. He'll do anything if you tell him you'll give him a baby. Then if you make a big fuss, he'll let you off the hook if you can guess his name. The simpleton still hasn't caught on that *everybody* knows his name.

(NICK *and* PUSS *cross to house.*)

NICK. Good day to you.

RUMPLESTILTSKIN & MRS. STILTSKIN. Good day.

NICK. You are the little man who spins straw into gold, are you not?

RUMPLESTILTSKIN. I am.

NICK. (*giving* RUMPLESTILTSKIN *the gold coin*) What can you tell us about this coin?

MRS. STILTSKIN. He doesn't work for free, you know. You must agree to pay him for his knowledge.

NICK. Certainly. What would you like?

(RUMPLESTILTSKIN *and* MRS. STILTSKIN *exchange looks.*)

RUMPLESTILTSKIN. I don't suppose you have a…oh, I don't know…baby on you?

NICK. No, but I'm sure I can get one.

PUSS. Where're you going to get a baby?

NICK. *(speaking Pig-Latin to* **PUSS***)* Ix-nay on the aby-bay. Remember – every-ay ody-bay ows-nay is-hay ame-nay.

PUSS. *(remembering)* Oh, right. *(confidently to* **RUMPLES-TILTSKIN***)* He can get a baby.

RUMPLESTILTSKIN. Excellent. Then, I shall be most happy to tell you whatever I can.

MRS. STILTSKIN. *(with a look at* **RUMPLESTILTSKIN***)* Perhaps we should have some refreshment to seal the bargain. You two look like you could use a cold drink.

NICK. Aren't you just the sweetest thing?

(**MRS. STILTSKIN** *exits into house.)*

RUMPLESTILTSKIN. *(looking at the coin)* What's so important about this coin anyway?

NICK. Oh, nothing. It's just that we…uh, we found it and uh…

PUSS. We're coin collectors!

NICK. Yes and we want to add it to our collection and so naturally we'd like to know something about it.

RUMPLESTILTSKIN. Not much to tell, really. It's from a Royal Treasury.

NICK. How can you tell?

RUMPLESTILTSKIN. See that letter on the back?

NICK. It looks like a "C" with a squiggle on top.

RUMPLESTILTSKIN. And what's the squiggle look like?

PUSS. A crown?

RUMPLESTILTSKIN. Exactly.

(*Enter* **MRS. STILTSKIN** *with a tray bearing four cups. She pours something from a vial into two of the cups.)*

NICK. So some royal person…

RUMPLESTILTSKIN. …whose name starts with a…

PUSS. "C?"

RUMPLESTILTSKIN. …had this made in their treasury. And not too long ago, either.

PUSS. How do you know that?

RUMPLESTILTSKIN. There's not a mark or scratch on it. It's brand new.

NICK. *(taking back coin)* Hmmm…that's very interesting.

MRS. STILTSKIN. Here we are! A nice cool drink! *(as NICK and PUSS reach for a glass)* No, not that one. No, the other one. Yes, could you take…no, yours are on the left…that's it!

(Everyone has a glass.)

MRS. STILTSKIN. Dear, how about a toast?

RUMPLESTILTSKIN. Over the teeth, past the gums, look out stomach, here she comes!

MRS. STILTSKIN. I was thinking more along the lines of "Your fate is sealed."

NICK. That's an odd toast but you're buying…

ALL. Your fate is sealed!

(Everyone drinks.)

NICK. Mmmm!

PUSS. Delicious!

(NICK and PUSS return cups to MRS. STILTSKIN. MRS. STILTSKIN and RUMPLESTILTSKIN exchange looks.)

MRS. STILTSKIN. Ah ha! You've fallen into our trap! We've told you what you want to know and now you must give us a baby.

(NICK exchanges looks with PUSS.)

NICK. What about letting me off the hook if I can guess your name? Isn't that how it usually works?

MRS. STILTSKIN. *(pretending to be disappointed)* Oh, you know about that, do you?

RUMPLESTILTSKIN. *(pretending to be disappointed)* If you insist. And I suppose you know exactly what my name is, just like everybody else.

NICK. Yes I do! It's…it's…

(The potion takes effect.)

NICK. *(He can't think of it and turns to **PUSS**.)* What were we just talking about?

PUSS. Who are you?

NICK. I don't know. Who are you?

MRS. STILTSKIN. The magic amnesia potion you drank has worked perfectly! You can't remember my husband's name and so you must give us a baby!

NICK. I have got to stop drinking everything people offer me!

PUSS. You cheated us!

MRS. STILTSKIN. Only because you tried to cheat us! Now hand over that baby, mister!

NICK. *(to **PUSS**)* Can you remember his name?

PUSS. No! Can you?

NICK. No! Now where am I going to get a baby?

PUSS. Don't look at me! If only someone around here could help us! *(notices audience)* Hey! What about those people?

NICK. Yes! Perfect! Maybe they have a baby we can give him!

PUSS. No! I mean maybe they know his name!

NICK. Ohhh! *(to audience)* Help! Do you know his name?

(They wait for audience to shout out "Rumplestiltskin!")

NICK & PUSS. What?

("Rumplestiltskin!")

NICK & PUSS. What?!

("Rumplestiltskin!")

NICK & PUSS. Rumplestiltskin!

RUMPLESTILTSKIN & MRS. STILTSKIN. Drat and blast!

MRS. STILTSKIN. *(stamping her foot)* I still have no baby!

RUMPLESTILTSKIN. That's not my fault!

(RUMPLESTILTSKIN *and* MRS. STILTSKIN *exit with house, still arguing.*)

PUSS. Wait! What about our memories?

NICK. Maybe there's a spell to restore them.

PUSS. But we don't know what it is! *(to audience)* I don't suppose you know a spell that could help us.

(They wait for the audience to chant the spell. Memories are restored.)

NICK. Phew! That was a close one! Thanks, partners!

PUSS. It's a good thing they're working with us or we'd be done for.

NICK. I hope you'll stop me from drinking anything harmful again. Hmm…where to next, do you suppose?

PUSS. There's another scene to this crime that we haven't checked yet. *(to audience)* Where did the pirates leave Granny Possum? *(waits for answer)*

NICK. *(snapping his fingers)* That's right! The beanstalk!

PUSS. I think we should sniff around there to see if we can find any more clues.

NICK. Me-ow! You are one clever kitten.

(NICK *and* PUSS *exit.*)

(Out [or down] comes the beanstalk. Enter FAIRY GOD-MOTHER *and* CINDERELLA *who has been changed into a cow.*)

FAIRY GODMOTHER. There! How does that feel? Glass slipper's on the other foot now, isn't it. Can't do much complaining when all you can say is…

COW. Moo.

(Opposite, enter NICK *and* PUSS.*)*

(NICK *and* PUSS *cross to* FAIRY GODMOTHER.*)*

PUSS. Fairy Godmother! How are you?

FAIRY GODMOTHER. Puss In Boots! Long time no see! I'm fine. And you?

PUSS. I'm good.

FAIRY GODMOTHER. *(to* **NICK***)* And you're…

NICK. Nick…

FAIRY GODMOTHER. …Tickle, the detective, right. We've met a few times.

NICK. *(meaning* **COW***)* Who's your friend?

FAIRY GODMOTHER. Oh, nobody. Just a cow I found wandering around. I thought she might belong to Jack so I brought her over.

COW. Moooooooooo!

NICK. Really? Because it looks sort of like…Cinderella… to me.

COW. Moo!

FAIRY GODMOTHER. Really? Cinderella? *(laughs)* I don't see it.

NICK. Maybe not. Because you'd never change Cinderella into a cow, would you.

PUSS. Of course she wouldn't.

FAIRY GODMOTHER. Of course I wouldn't. Why would I do that?

NICK. I don't know. It sounds crazy.

FAIRY GODMOTHER. It sounds totally crazy!

COW. Moo!

(a pause)

NICK. It is Cinderella, isn't it.

(a pause)

FAIRY GODMOTHER. Yes.

NICK. Why would you…

FAIRY GODMOTHER. To teach her some gratitude! She's always complaining! Why don't I show up earlier? Why don't I punish her step-mother and step-sisters? Why does she have to be home by midnight? She never shuts up, the ungrateful thing!

NICK. Change her back.

FAIRY GODMOTHER. After everything I do for her…!

NICK. Change her back.

FAIRY GODMOTHER. Very well.

(**FAIRY GODMOTHER** *changes* **COW** *back into* **CINDER-ELLA.**)

CINDERELLA. I bet you thought that was very funny, didn't you.

FAIRY GODMOTHER. Yes, actually. But I only wanted to…

CINDERELLA. Teach me some gratitude, yeah, I heard. Just wait until the Fairy Godmother Council hears about this.

FAIRY GODMOTHER. *(scared)* You won't tell them, will you?

CINDERELLA. Try and stop me.

(**FAIRY GODMOTHER** *raises her wand.*)

PUSS. *(to* **CINDERELLA***)* Girlfriend, unless you want to be a cow again, I'd zip it.

NICK. I don't mean to interrupt but how long have you two been here?

FAIRY GODMOTHER. Just a few minutes. And we'd've been gone by now if you two meddling kids hadn't come along. Why?

NICK. Have you seen anything odd?

CINDERELLA. *(with a look at* **FAIRY GODMOTHER***)* You mean anything odder than a girl turned into a cow?

FAIRY GODMOTHER. No.

CINDERELLA. Maybe you should ask the horse that was here earlier.

NICK. What horse?

CINDERELLA. *(pointing to the ground)* The horse that made those hoof prints.

NICK. Aren't they yours?

CINDERELLA. *(offended)* Hardly. Horse prints and cow prints look totally different. And these have been here for a while. A few hours, at least.

FAIRY GODMOTHER. How would you know that?

CINDERELLA. Duh – I have to take care of the animals on our farm. Which I wouldn't if you'd come around sooner.

(**FAIRY GODMOTHER** *raises her wand.*)

PUSS. *(hurriedly)* Do you think they're a clue?

NICK. Since I didn't see any horses at the pirate ship, they must have come from the person who took Granny Possum away! *(following the trail of hoof prints)* And they lead in this direction.

FAIRY GODMOTHER. There you go, complaining again. It takes some effort on my part to make your dreams come true, you know.

CINDERELLA. Yeah, whatever.

FAIRY GODMOTHER. It's that bad attitude that got you turned into a cow.

CINDERELLA. *(mimicking her)* It's that bad attitude that got you turned into a cow.

FAIRY GODMOTHER. See? There's that tone of voice I warned you about.

CINDERELLA. *(mimicking her)* See? There's that tone of voice I warned you about!

GIANT. *(off)* Who's making that racket down there?!

PUSS. *(looking up)* The giant!

CINDERELLA. *(looking up)* Oh, mind your own business!

NICK. *(looking up)* Let's not stick around – I think things are going to get ugly!

PUSS. Some people just don't know when to keep quiet.

(**NICK** *and* **PUSS** *turn to follow the "trail."*)

FAIRY GODMOTHER. Speaking of keeping quiet…you two won't tell the Fairy Godmother Council on me, will you?

NICK. Well, I don't know…

PUSS. I don't think she meant any harm.

FAIRY GODMOTHER. I really didn't!

PUSS. And she's under a lot of strain…

FAIRY GODMOTHER. Oh, I am, I am!

CINDERELLA. Don't listen to her! We could get her into lots of trouble! We could teach *her* a lesson for a change!

(**FAIRY GODMOTHER** *draws away a bit and pulls out a small vial.*)

NICK. I'm not looking to get anyone into trouble…

PUSS. It is the first time she's ever done anything like this. I think we should let her off the hook.

CINDERELLA. Oh, so I'm the only one has to be punished around here? I like that! That's really fair!

FAIRY GODMOTHER. *(to herself)* One sip of this amnesia potion and I won't have to worry about a thing!

PUSS. No one ever said life was fair.

CINDERELLA. Yes they did! Everyone who ever told one of our stories says life is fair! Play by the rules and everything will turn out okay! But that's not how life works!

PUSS. That's how your life works – you marry a Prince.

CINDERELLA. I was just turned into a cow!

NICK. Look, I don't want to get into a philosophical discussion here…

FAIRY GODMOTHER. *(rejoining group)* You all look so thirsty. How about a little something to drink? This is a very special refreshment made by a friend who lives in a candy house.

NICK. I always enjoy a tasty beverage.

(**NICK** *is about to drink when hopefully the plant in the audience will stop him and others will join in.*)

NICK. What? I shouldn't drink it? Why not? Another amnesia potion from the witch? *(to* **FAIRY GODMOTHER***)* Hey, what are you trying to pull here?

FAIRY GODMOTHER. I just wanted to make sure I wouldn't get into trouble for one little mistake. Can't you give me a second chance?

PUSS. Everyone deserves a second chance. Don't worry, we won't say anything about this to anyone…

NICK. …if you promise not to do it again.

FAIRY GODMOTHER. I promise I will never turn Cinderella into a cow again.

PUSS. That's good enough for me.

CINDERELLA. This is so typical!

NICK. Sorry to run, ladies, but we're hot on the trail of a kidnapper and we don't have a minute to lose. *(to* CINDERELLA*)* You be good… *(to* FAIRY GODMOTHER*)* …and you be good. No more cows!

FAIRY GODMOTHER. No more cows.

PUSS. Thanks for your help!

(NICK *and* PUSS *quickly exit following the trail. Perhaps They follow it through the audience.)*

(FAIRY GODMOTHER *and* CINDERELLA *start to exit.)*

CINDERELLA. I don't believe this! Everyone is so unfair to blondes just because we have more fun! Blonde persecution!

FAIRY GODMOTHER. You're making me angry again.

CINDERELLA. Oh, I'm so scared.

FAIRY GODMOTHER. I promised I wouldn't turn you into a cow. There are a lot of worse things you could be than a cow.

CINDERELLA. I'd like to see you try it!

(CINDERELLA *exits.)*

FAIRY GODMOTHER. *(waving her wand to* CINDERELLA *off)* Alla-kazam!

CINDERELLA. *(off)* Aaaaaaahhhhhhhh!

FAIRY GODMOTHER. Told you!

GIANT. *(off)* Don't make me come down there!

(FAIRY GODMOTHER *exits [taking beanstalk if need be].)*

(NICK *and* PUSS *enter.)*

PUSS. So what do we know?

NICK. Someone with access to a royal treasury who rides a horse hired Bluebeard and his men to kidnap Granny Possum. But why? We still don't know why.

PUSS. It is a puzzlement.

NICK. I wonder if anything out of the ordinary happened when Granny came into her clearing today. Maybe she saw something unusual and the kidnapper wanted to keep her quiet. If only someone had seen her when she came by…

(**NICK** *is trying to get the audience to tell about* **GRANNY** *taking the pages out of her book and balling them up and tossing them away.*)

NICK. She ripped some pages out of her book? Can I see them?

(**NICK** *and* **PUSS** *look at the pages.*)

NICK. It's all about Prince Charming.

PUSS. I've never heard this story before. He usually just comes in at the end, and kisses somebody or puts a glass slipper on somebody's foot and Goodnight, Marie. Do you think this means anything?

NICK. There's that mark again on the back. Where have I seen it before? What other papers have we seen today? *(waits for audience to remind him of the ransom note and note to pirates)*

(**NICK** *takes out notes.*)

NICK. Yes! It's the same one on the ransom note and the note to the pirates.

PUSS. I think we've seen it somewhere else – the letter "C" with a crown on top. Does anyone remember where else we've seen it? *(waits for audience to suggest gold coin)* Right! On the gold coin! Rumplestiltskin talked about it.

(**NICK** *takes out coin, compares the "C."*)

NICK. It's the same as the others. Hmmm, I think I know who our kidnapper is and where these hoof prints are leading. *(to audience)* Who do you suspect? *(waits for*

answers from audience) There's only one way to find out
– follow the trail. But we'll have to go in disguise. *(to
audience)* You follow the tracks and we'll meet you…
where they end.

(**NICK** *and* **PUSS** *exit.*)

(Enter **WAYNE** *and* **BERT**, *palace guards, carrying
spears. They bring on the castle door that they guard.)*

BERT. Castle Guard First Class Wayne Gunderson?

WAYNE. That's me.

BERT. Bert Parrot, reporting for duty as ordered, sir.

WAYNE. Bert Parrot. First day as a palace guard, eh, Parrot?

BERT. Yes, sir.

WAYNE. Not scared, are you, Parrot?

BERT. No, sir. Well, maybe a little, sir.

WAYNE. Don't worry. I'll teach you everything you need to
know.

BERT. Thank you, sir.

WAYNE. I've been a guard here for 37 years and I know
every last thing there is to know about guarding.

BERT. Permission to "huzzah," sir?

WAYNE. Permission granted.

BERT. Huzzah!

WAYNE. Now, first thing, let's see your angry face.

BERT. My what, sir?

WAYNE. Your angry face. When you're on duty, you've got
to have an angry face to show folks you mean business.
Let's see it.

(**BERT** *tries a face.*)

WAYNE. No, no, that'll never do. Look at me.

(**WAYNE** *does a face.*)

WAYNE. See that? Now try it again.

(**BERT** *tries another face.*)

WAYNE. Is that the best you've got?

(**BERT** *tries another face.*)

WAYNE. Better. We'll work on it. Now do your angry face again and this time, add a fearsome growl.

BERT. Fearsome growl, sir?

WAYNE. Whenever anyone threatens you or gives you trouble, you do your angry face *and* your fearsome growl to take the spirit out of them and show 'em who's boss. Works every time. Let me hear it.

(**BERT** *gives a tiny growl.*)

WAYNE. Did someone let a little kitty cat in here? I thought I heard a kitty crying.

(**BERT** *gives a louder growl.*)

WAYNE. Really? That wouldn't frighten a child. Now, listen.

(**WAYNE** *gives a momentous fearsome growl.*)

WAYNE. (*with his angry face, right up close to* **BERT**) Now give it to me!

(**BERT** *gives a terrible growl and makes a most horrible face. It scares* **WAYNE**.)

WAYNE. That's more like it!

(*Enter* **NICK** *and* **PUSS**. **NICK** *is dressed as a female rat catcher with Puss's sword hidden under his skirt.* **PUSS** *tries to look like an innocent cat without her hat and boots.*)

NICK. (*to audience, showing off the rat pelts hanging from his belt*) How do you like my dead rats? Nobody'll recognize me in this get-up so we should be able to get into the castle and rescue Granny Possum without any trouble.

PUSS. I feel naked without my hat and boots.

NICK. Just try to act like a regular cat.

PUSS. But I'm not a regular cat. I'm…

NICK. Shhh! I know, you're Puss in Boots, but for the next few minutes, you're a regular cat named Muffin. Come on.

(**NICK** *and* **PUSS** *cross to guards.*)

WAYNE. *(with his angry face)* Halt!

BERT. Who goes there?

WAYNE. Angry face.

BERT. *(with his angry face)* Who goes there?

NICK. *(in a female voice)* It's just me, Bertha Rat Catcher… *(He indicates the rat pelts and then* **PUSS.***)* …and my best rat-catching cat, Muffin.

PUSS. Meow!

WAYNE. State your business.

NICK. Prince Charming sent for us. Seems he's having a little rat problem and he'd like us to attend to it toot-suite.

WAYNE. *(with a fearsome growl)* Is that so?

BERT. Nobody told us about it.

NICK. Oh, I daresay it's too trivial a matter to bother such high-ranking guards with. I'm sure you have much more important things to deal with.

BERT. *(flattered)* Well, uh, yeah, I'm sure we do. Don't we?

WAYNE. Of course we do. Lots of uhm…important stuff we've got to be thinking about…

NICK. Perhaps you'd be kind enough to escort a simple, old woman and her cat to the Prince's private chambers.

WAYNE. We'd be delighted!

BERT. Least we can do for someone the Prince sent for special.

WAYNE. Wait! *(angry face)* How do we know the Prince really sent for you?

(**NICK** *takes out the papers and shows the "C" on the back.*)

NICK. Isn't this his very own personal stationery? "C" for Charming? And the little crown on top?

WAYNE. Why, so it is. No one uses it but the Prince himself.

NICK. *(taking out the gold coin)* And didn't he pay me with this new gold coin?

BERT. It's so new he must have taken it directly from his royal treasury. I guess he really did send for you. Right this way, Bertha.

NICK. How lovely. Come along, Muffin.

PUSS. Meow!

*(**BERT**, **WAYNE**, **NICK** and **PUSS** go through the castle door and begin to slowly walk through the "castle halls.")*

*(During this, the "Prince's chambers" are brought out. Primarily, there should be a door to knock on and "inside," an area hidden by a curtain behind which **GRANNY POSSUM** sits on a stool. **PRINCE CHARMING** is in his room before the curtain.)*

NICK. What a huge castle! I'm surprised you don't have to ride a horse to get from one place to another.

WAYNE. The only horses around here are owned by the Prince.

BERT. And he's the only one allowed to ride them.

NICK. You certainly know a lot about the Prince.

BERT. It's hard not to. He talks about himself all the time.

WAYNE. He's mad that whenever he's in a story, he just rides in at the end. He says he's tired that no one ever tells *his* story so he has to do it himself. Here we are!

*(They have arrived at the Prince's chambers. **WAYNE** knocks on the door.)*

WAYNE. Your Majesty! We've brought the rat catcher you sent for.

PRINCE CHARMING. Rat catcher? I didn't send for any rat catcher.

*(**PRINCE CHARMING** opens the door. **NICK** brushes past and enters room.)*

NICK. What a lovely room you have, Your Highness. Isn't it nice, Muffin?

PUSS. Meow!

PRINCE CHARMING. See here! You'll have to leave! I don't have any rats that need catching.

NICK. Oh, I think there's a great big rat in here and I'm about to catch him good and proper!

PRINCE CHARMING. Guards, seize this crazy old woman and throw her out!

(BURT *and* WAYNE *do their angry faces and their fearsome growls and move toward* NICK, *but he whips out the sword and tosses it to* PUSS *who stands, catches it and uses it to keep the* GUARDS *at bay.*)

PUSS. I may not be wearing them but I am most certainly… Puss In Boots! Cross swords with me if you dare!

(PUSS *does her angry face and fearsome growl and the* BURT *and* WAYNE *cower.*)

BURT. Now that's what I was talking about!

PRINCE CHARMING. Here now! What do you think you're doing? I'll see you in the dungeon for this!

NICK. At least I'll have you for company when everyone finds out that you…kidnapped Granny Possum!

(NICK *flings the curtain aside and we see* GRANNY POSSUM *sitting on a stool calmly knitting.*)

GRANNY POSSUM. (*pleasantly*) Hello, dear. My, you've got some lovely rats there, haven't you.

NICK. (*tearing off his disguise*) Granny, it's me, Nick Tickle! I've come to rescue you!

GRANNY POSSUM. But I don't want to be rescued.

NICK. You're welcome! Wait! What?! Why not?

GRANNY POSSUM. Because it's very agreeable here and the Prince has been very kind to me. Look at the afghan I'm making for him. (*She holds up her knitting.*)

NICK. Are you kidding me? I've been running around like crazy trying to find you! The pirates tickled me and Rumplestiltskin poisoned me and Bluebeard almost killed me and now it turns out you don't want to be rescued?! Listen, lady, I've come to rescue you and whether you want to be rescued or not, you're going to be rescued!

GRANNY POSSUM. But I don't need to be rescued. The Prince already rescued me from those terrible pirates and now I'm a guest in his castle. I could leave right now if I wanted to but I've decided to stay.

NICK. But we need you to tell the stories!

GRANNY POSSUM. I'm tired of telling the stories. Let someone else do it for a change. Prince Charming says I need a vacation and I can stay here as long as I like.

NICK. But Prince Charming is the one who paid the pirates to kidnap you in the first place!

GRANNY POSSUM. *(shocked, to* **PRINCE CHARMING***)* Is that true?

PRINCE CHARMING. *(mumbling)* Maybe...

GRANNY POSSUM. Why did you want me kidnapped?

PRINCE CHARMING. So I could tell my story for once! No one ever gets to hear about me. You only ever tell about Sleeping Beauty and Snow White and Cinderella.

GRANNY POSSUM. Is that why I found those pages about you in my book? (**PRINCE CHARMING** *nods.)* Well, I suppose there's been no real harm done but you've been very naughty and you have to be punished.

PUSS. We could put him in the dungeon.

PRINCE CHARMING. *(horrified)* Not that!

NICK. We could tell his wife. *(calling)* Snow White!

PRINCE CHARMING. *(even more horrified)* I'll take the dungeon!

GRANNY POSSUM. I think not telling his story will be punishment enough.

PRINCE CHARMING. Never?!

GRANNY POSSUM. Well, at least for...

PUSS. A year and a day.

GRANNY POSSUM. A year and day it is. After that, I'll be happy to tell everyone all about you.

NICK. So does this mean that you're going back on the job?

GRANNY POSSUM. *(with a big sigh)* You're sure someone else couldn't tell the stories for a while?

PUSS. No!

NICK. Everyone likes the way you do it. *(to audience)* Don't you?

*(***NICK*** *encourages the audience to vocalize their desire to have her return.)*

GRANNY POSSUM. *(touched)* Well, I didn't realize everyone cared so much. If that's how they feel, I suppose I must go back to work.

PUSS. Congratulations, Nick. You've solved the mystery and now everything's back to normal.

NICK. Thanks to you and all my partners out there. *(to audience)* Well done, Junior Detectives! Give yourselves a hand.

PUSS. *(licking her lips)* If we're all finished here, I'd be happy to take care of those delicious rats for you…

NICK. One last thing to do. Since she didn't get to say it earlier, I think she should say it now. Go ahead, Granny Possum.

GRANNY. Let's do it altogether, shall we? *(taking center stage and clearing her voice)* And so we all lived…*(everyone says:)* happily ever after!

(curtain)

PROP LIST

Large storybook
Extra pages
Mirror frame
Basket of flower petals
Picnic basket
Cake
Blanket
Heart
Deck of cards
Ugly witch mask
Basket of apples
Bad apple (prune? plum?)
Hobby horse
Breath spray
Ransom note
Lollypop
Pouch
Coins silver and gold
Assorted swords
Mugs
Pirate note
Broom
2 Vials
Tray
4 Glasses
Fairy wand
2 Spears
Belt of dead rat pelts
Piece of knitting with 2 knitting needles

COSTUME LIST

GRANNY - Dress, shawl, perhaps a bonnet
QUEEN - Robe, crown, disguise cape
MIRROR - Bright pants and shirt
SNOW WHITE - Long dress or robe
VINNIE - shirt, pants, vest, tie, fedora
STEVE - Bright pants, shirt, perhaps a vest, funny hat
MERLE - Bright pants, shirt, perhaps a vest, funny hat
PRINCE - Shirt, pants, cape, crown
BLUEBEARD - Shirt, pants, vest, captain's hat
PIRATE - Ragged shirt and pants, kerchief
NICK - Pants, shirt, tie, trench coat, fedora
PUSS - Tights, bodice or shirt, boots, jaunty hat
RUMPLESTILTSKIN - Funny pants, shirt, hat
MRS. STILTSKIN - Funny dress, apron
FAIRY GODMOTHER - Gown or robe, wings, perhaps a pointy hat
CINDERELLA - Dress, "cow" head-covering or similar disguise
WAYNE - Pants, shirt, tunic, guard helmet
BERT - Pants, shirt, tunic, guard helmet

AUTHOR'S NOTE

If the two dwarves are both women, the following lines should be used in the mirror's speech (page 18)

She's living with two tiny maids

In one of the forest's leafy glades.

If the two dwarves are played by one guy and one gal, the following lines should be used:

She's living with two tiny folk

Out in the forest – this ain't no joke.

Also by
Steph DeFerie...

Once Upon a Wolf

After the Rain King

Emmalina Scrooge

Ghost Rider

A Play About A Dragon

Return of the King

Please visit our website **bakersplays.com** for complete
descriptions and licensing information

OTHER TITLES AVAILABLE FROM BAKER'S PLAYS

ONCE UPON A WOLF

Steph DeFerie

Comedy / 2f / 2m each playing multiple roles / simple props, costumes, set

This fast and furious collection of fractured fairy tales with a modern twist tells what happens when the Big Bad Wolf decides he (or she) doesn't want to be big or bad anymore! Old Granny Stinkyfeet is just trying to tell the kiddies some stories but she's having trouble with the Wolf. He won't eat her like he's supposed to! Instead, he wants to be the good guy for a change, so he's off on a mission to become a hero – no matter how many people tell him it's impossible. The show utilizes audience participation.

www.ingramcontent.com/pod-product-compliance
Lightning Source LLC
Chambersburg PA
CBHW061054050726
47592CB00004B/1677